Published by Ladybird Books Ltd 2010
A Penguin Company
Penguin Books Ltd, 80 Strand, London, WC2R 0RL, UK
Penguin Books Australia Ltd, Camberwell, Victoria, Australia
Penguin Books (NZ), 67 Apollo Drive, Rosedale, North Shore
0632, New Zealand (a divison of Pearson New Zealand Ltd)

www.ladybird.com

Printed in China

This book is based on the
TV Series 'Peppa Pig'
'Peppa Pig' is created by
Neville Astley and Mark Baker

www.peppapig.com

The story of Peppa Pig

My Family Tree

by Peppa Pig

Once upon a time, there was a loveable, slightly bossy little piggy, named Peppa.

Grunt!
Grunt!

More than anything in the whole wide world,
Peppa loved jumping **UP** and **DOWN** in muddy puddles.

Mummy Pig was Peppa's mummy.
She was *very* wise about most things.
Mummy Pig would say,
"Peppa, when you jump in muddy
puddles, you must wear your boots."

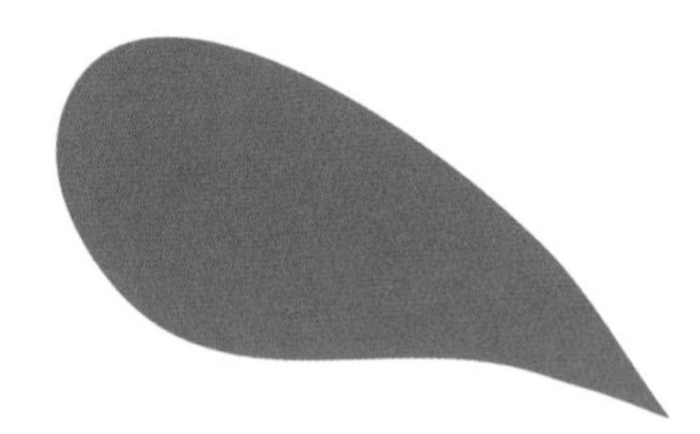

Daddy Pig was Peppa's daddy. He loved eating cookies and he had a big round tummy. When Daddy Pig jumped in muddy puddles, he made a very **big** muddy splash.

When Peppa's little brother George was born,
Peppa helped look after him.

And as soon as George was old enough, Peppa taught him how to jump in muddy puddles. "George!" Peppa said, just like Mummy Pig. "If you jump in muddy puddles, you must wear your boots."

Squelch!

Squelch!

George liked muddy puddles, but he liked his toy, Mr Dinosaur more. Even though George couldn't speak yet, he could say one very word, *very* well . . .

Sometimes Peppa got a little bit annoyed with George. "George," she would sigh, "why do you ALWAYS say dine-saw for everything? It's soooo boring!"

One day, Peppa, George, Mummy and Daddy Pig got into their little car and drove to their new house on top of a little green hill. Peppa was excited about the new house, but she was **very** excited about the very wet and extremely muddy puddles in the garden!

"Can we go and jump in the muddy puddles?" asked Peppa. "It's nearly time for bed, Peppa," replied Mummy. "You'll have to wait until tomorrow."

Peppa and George woke up very early the next morning and went to find Mummy and Daddy Pig.

“Can we *please* go outside and jump in muddy puddles?” asked Peppa, excitedly.

“We’re going to Granny and Grandpa Pig’s house today, Peppa,” replied Mummy Pig, sleepily. “You can jump in muddy puddles there.”

After breakfast, it was time to leave, so Peppa and her family jumped into their little car. "Ready?" asked Daddy Pig, cheerily. "Yes, Daddy Pig!" everyone answered back. "Then, let's **GO!!!**" shouted Daddy Pig.

"**Yippee!**" cried Peppa. She couldn't wait to get to Granny and Grandpa Pig's house and jump in muddy puddles.

The family soon arrived at Granny and Grandpa's house. Peppa and George were very excited. They loved going to visit Granny and Grandpa Pig.

"Granny Pig, Grandpa Pig!" cried Peppa.
"Gangy Ig, Baba Ig!" shouted George.
"Hello, my little ones!" answered Granny Pig. "Come inside."
"Granny," said Peppa. "Can I jump in muddy puddles please?"

“I think Grandpa Pig has something to show you first, Peppa,” said Granny Pig. Peppa was a little disappointed. She really wanted to jump in muddy puddles.

Grandpa Pig took Peppa and George to his vegetable garden.
"This is where I grow my vegetables," said Grandpa Pig.
"First I plant some seeds . . ."
"Can we eat your yummy vegetables, Grandpa?" asked Peppa, forgetting all about muddy puddles.
"We have to wait for them to grow a bit bigger," replied Grandpa.
"Ooooooh!" gasped Peppa, excitedly.

Snort! Snort!
Ved-gees!

Suddenly, there was a loud **BANG**!
"Oh dear!" gasped Grandpa Pig.
"That was thunder. That means it's going to rain.
We should hurry inside before we get wet."

Peppa, George and Grandpa Pig ran inside
as fast as they could to get out of the rain.

Peppa and George
watched the rain
splish-splash-splosh
down the window.
George started to cry.
"Don't cry, George,"
said Peppa. "It's only rain."

Dine-saw!

But George wasn't crying because it was raining. George was crying because he had *lost* Mr Dinosaur.

Peppa searched upstairs . . .

downstairs . . .

and *even* in the toilet . . .

but she couldn't find Mr Dinosaur anywhere. Just then, she had an idea . . .

Peppa ran outside and found a *very* wet Mr Dinosaur in Grandpa's *very* muddy vegetable garden.

She ran inside and gave Mr Dinosaur to George. George was very happy.

"The rain has stopped," cried Peppa. "What can we do, now?"
"I have a very good idea, Peppa," said Daddy Pig, pointing outside.

"Hooray!" cheered Peppa, seeing the muddiest puddles ever. Peppa had been so busy looking at Grandpa's vegetables and searching for Mr Dinosaur, she had forgotten all about jumping in puddles.

Grunt! Grunt!

Grunt! Grunt!

Squelch!

Squelch!

Peppa loved jumping up and down in muddy puddles more than anything in the whole wide world. All of Peppa's family loved jumping up and down in muddy puddles more than anything in the whole wide world.

Hee! Hee! Ha! Ha! Oink! Oink!

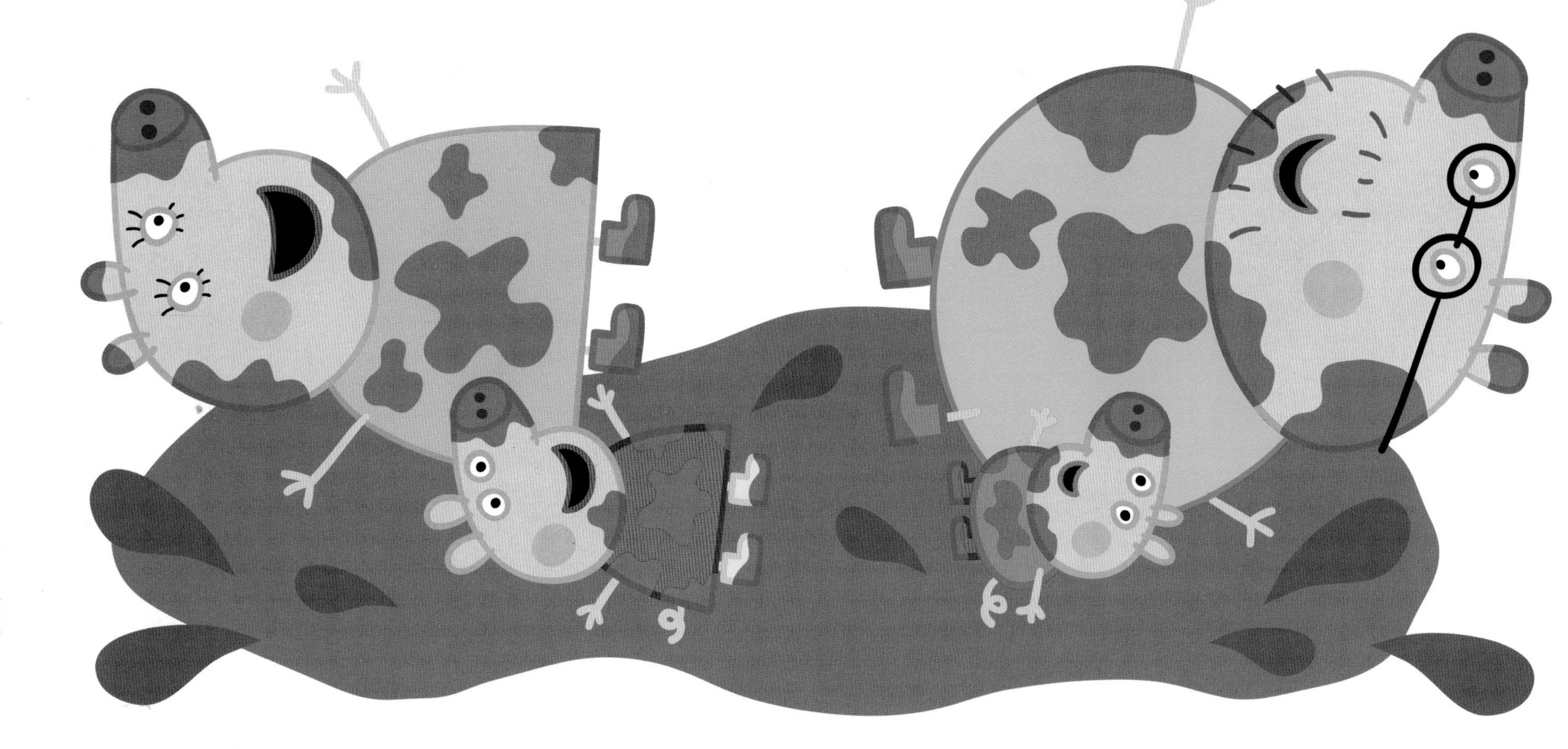

Hee! Hee! Hee! Ha! Ha! Grunt! Snort!